DIMINISHED HARVEST

DR. WANDA D. TOLBERT

Book III

This is the third book of my Harvest Series. The first book The Harvest Is Past, The Summer Is Ended, and we Are Not Saved tells the life of several school friends, some are Christians, and some are not, but they attend the same private Christian school. The story tells some of the various things that happen at school with the students that make some kids think salvation doesn't mean a thing and it isn't worth going to church, but before the end of the summer, they find out differently! The story is intriguing and will have you on a surprising journey!

Harvest of The Remnant is the sequel and it continues to tell the life story of several friends who continue to go to school together. The story continues to be intriguing and will have you ready to continue reading and turning to the next page too see if what you are already thinking is about to happen!

Diminished Harvest is the third book of this series. It focuses on when the friends are getting out of high school and what happens next. Some will stay on the high road while some take the low road with some even finding themselves climbing out of a gutter of sin and shame! Will they make it, or is the Harvest totally diminished?

Chapter 1

Looking Back

I never forget to thank God for sparing my life back in school. I can't believe how the time has gone by when some of our classmates died in a fire during summer camp. Quite a few of them that survived and repented start going to church. As the time went on most of them stopped and start enjoying their life again as they would call it. They forgot how close they came to death and now they wanted to enjoy their life. Sorry to say it meant they didn't include God in their enjoyment, they start thinking going to church was boring and useless again. They had better stuff to do and were just too busy. Darius however continued to go and he had joined Malik's dad's church and start getting involved in ministry. It started paying off for him too how we had to learn and recite a scripture a week. It really helped him when he started witnessing to people, he did it effectively! He actually led Matt's parents to Christ! He never stopped visiting them after their son had died at camp that summer. He also started going back and trying to get people we had went to school with to visit church. Some had graduated from college, some had start working right out of school and some had got married and even had a couple of kids already! Wow how time did go by! Darius start inviting so many people to church he became a serious soul winner!

Malik even asked his dad if they could pray and fast together about assigning him to an outreach ministry to win souls first…and help increase the church membership. After they both had received an answer from God they approached Darius, God had already touched his heart as well! He said he kept feeling like he wanted to do something like this, but he didn't want anyone to think he was just going after a title. He also told them he didn't know if they thought he would be worthy of this position in church since he used to live a life in the beginning at school turning it up as he said. Malik's dad told him to never forget what it says in Philippians 3:13-14, Brethen, I count not myself to have apprehended: but this one thing I do, forgetting those things which are behind, and reaching forth unto those things which are before, I press toward the mark for the prize of the high calling in Christ Jesus. If God has put whatever it is for whomever in the sea of forgetfulness that's all that matters! Malik's dad told him some people never win a soul their whole life, or even invite anyone to church outside of their immediate family that live in the same house. We all should be soul winners, but people for whatever reason don't or are nervous about approaching people. Malik said dad let's keep it simple and call this ministry SSW for Serious Soul Winners! Darius got the ideal from Lillian the two of us had became good friends in college. She is still going through a healing process from being forced to get an abortion by her parents. She thought her life was over, especially when they made her come to the college where I was at and not attend Seminary as she always wanted too! They were so scared someone would find out she had gotten pregnant over the summer, and how it would affect their positions in church since they were ministry heads. Her ex-boyfriend had gotten someone else pregnant after her, but he married that girl, his parents thought this would slow him down sort of speak. And his parents believed she was the right one for his future ministry because of her parent's connections. But through all of this Lillian started PKID, Preachers Kids In Distress! Malik said she gave him the idea of just calling Darius ministry SSW.

Chapter 2

SSW

Darius already went out on Saturday mornings witnessing to people. He said why should the Mormons and Jehovah Witnesses be the only ones out? He said they were faithfully assigned by their leaders to do the work for their organizations that we should be doing with no one having to assign it to us in the first place. He said it was already a requirement that is if you were filled with the Holy Ghost. Just read Acts 1:8, But you shall received power, after the Holy Ghost is come upon you: and ye shall be witnesses unto me both in Jerusalem, and in all Judea, and in Samaria, and unto the uttermost part of the earth! He said that all most churches were doing were accepting lazy people who became lazy members. He said we should let people know we expect something out of them as members and they should expect something out of their Christian walk! It was time to just quit going to church and leaving out the same way you came in, never having any progress in your spiritual walk. Malik wanted the three of them to fast before launching off the new ministry. After they fasted they announced the ministry at service and everyone was excited.

Matt's parents told Darius they wanted to help and support him anyway they could! Luke had already joined Malik's church he was from one of the don't churches that Darius had invited. He had stopped going to his church because he felt like there was nothing to do and most of the young people were leaving anyway. He said at his church they sang the same old songs, the same people sang all the songs and they never let any new musicians play during the service. He had tried suggesting new and different things at church, but he always got turned down. He said he had just been praying, reading his bible and streaming services at home. A lot of the youth and young adults had left his church and some had even joined bands and were singing in clubs. So when Darius saw him out and invited him to a youth service he gave it a try. He said he couldn't believe how strongly he felt the presence of the Holy Spirit on him during service, but even before then how he felt welcomed by the greeters! He said at his church they had people at the door that would make people feel uncomfortable if they did not look presentable. It made me think of what my grandparents would always say you have to catch a fish first before you can clean it! Luke had encouraged his girlfriend Brittney to come. They had met at a coffee shop while he was in college and she was totally turned off at his old church. She felt like the sermon was about her, she wore make-up, jewelry and her skirt did not come down to her ankles. Luke tried to tell her the sermon wasn't about her, that's just what they were preaching that day. But the next time she visited it was more of the same and she never went back. She wasn't raised in church like Luke and when she told her parents what happened they said that's why they didn't go to church because churches were full of hypocrites. Luke asked her to just try giving God one more chance! He told her she didn't pass the bar the first time she took her exam, so why is she only giving God one chance? So she went and she enjoyed the service! Luke was thrilled because he knew he wanted to marry Brittney. His parents were hoping he would marry one of the girls from their church, but he told them most of the girls from his church looked the part but outside of the church they were different. He told them they might as well have been pole dancers they were so wild! And all they wanted to do was get married and have a bunch of kids and have someone take care of them he told them he wanted to marry someone he could build a life with and assist in building up Gods Kingdom on earth and adding up fruit to their account in heaven. His dad said he understood and his parents prayed that he would meet the right girl. When they met Brittney they thought she was decent and had a good head on her shoulders. Luke told them he had joined a ministry called SSW at church and Brittney said she would be joining also and going out on Saturdays helping Luke. Luke had asked her to go, and afterwards he would take her to lunch. He knew that was her favorite meal of the day! It was about 20 people that would be joining SSW including Malik. Luke had been one of the kids that went to Honduras on a missionary trip when we were in high school. He told Malik he really wanted to go to areas where Spanish people lived. Malik told him he didn't know that much Spanish. But Luke told him Brittney could speak in Spanish and he had kept in touch with Raquel. She also went on the trip to Honduras and her family was from Honduras. Luke contacted her and told her what they were doing. She thought it was a great idea! She was part of a Spanish Ministry and they didn't have assigned times that they would go out witnessing. She said she would just witness to people when she was out and about and invite people to church and give them a card. She said at her church they really didn't have any ministries for her age group. Malik's dad announced at church that during the next service they would lay hands on the people that were going to be in the SSW Ministry and asked for all those that were joining to do a 24 hour fast the day before the service because some things only happen with fasting and much prayer. He was serious about people of all ages been trained to properly serve God. He said we had to go to school, learn how to drive, and his mom joined the conversation before he could finish and said before all that we mom's know you have to be trained to go to the bathroom! His dad said he was sad to say in some churches you can just come and join a ministry just because they need help, or you have money and they don't care if you don't know what the heck you're doing or talking about! He said he promised God he wouldn't allow people to have zeal without knowledge in his church. He knew this could hurt the ministry. Luke's parents were coming and he asked Brittney to invite her parents but she said they would never come. So he asked them and said he would pick them up and they said they would come. Brittney couldn't believe it! Her dad said he wanted to see for himself what she was going to be a part of and make sure it was not some kind of cult, or hustle for money since everyone knew she was going to be an attorney. Her mom said she just wanted to come to be supportive of her. Luke didn't care why they said they would come. He had been praying for their salvation and knew this would be a step in the right direction!

Chapter 3

Laying on of Hands!

Before the service we all fasted, for some it was the first time they ever fasted. Some people met at the church to kick the fast off and pray. One person that was joining SSW said he knew Gandhi fasted to have freedom from being ruled by the British, Dr. Martin Luther King fasted for civil rights and Caesar Chavez fasted for the farm workers. But why did everybody have to fast to go out witnessing? Darius was the leader, he should just fast. The pastor told him this was part of the problem in churches. No one knows their potential worth. We should all be ministers and flames of fire. And he also told him one could chase a thousand and two could put ten thousand to flight, we would join forces together. There were was so many teens that did nothing at church, and they grew into young adults who didn't participate at church. Do you have to wait until you are senior citizens before you can be active or a strong leader in church? There was a big crowd that day at church because everyone had invited family members and there was a light lunch afterwards. Lillian and I were there as well to be supportive. Luke told her he heard how she was treated at her old church and said he was sorry they treated her like that. He told her he would be praying for her ministry as well because sometimes it seems that kids that grow up in church with their parents in ministry have added pressure on them to be perfect. It seems like they never get to run or plan their own life. They are expected to follow in their parents footsteps. Another girl that had left the church Lillian went to was there as well. She asked her to meet her for coffee the next day. She told me she didn't want to meet her, but the girl was persistence.

They met on her lunch break the next day and she apologized for snubbing her like other people. She said there were so many rumors going around she just believed what she heard and was told instead of finding out if any truth was behind it. She told her she found out that her ex-boyfriend had married his wife because she was pregnant, but he later found out it wasn't even his baby! They had 2 more after the first one, those were his. She knew this information because she was engaged to his best friend. They had been dating for a while and were planning their wedding. They would go out to eat sometimes with her old boyfriend and his wife and her old boyfriend seemed unattached. She told her he wanted to get a divorce, but his parents were furious, they said people may not accept him with blemishes on his record and to make the best of it. They did not care how unhappy he was. And they said they were too attached to the oldest son by now, he was their grandchild. She said he was going from job to job, and had started drinking heavily and he was sleeping around on his wife now. She said his wife had start trying to get her life back together spiritually and that's another reason she felt like his parents wanted them to stay together, plus her parents were getting their son a position to travel with a television personality during the summer. His parents thought this was a great idea since he was in-between jobs and it could help kick off his screen time ministry.

Their daughter-in-law didn't work so they helped support them. Lillian told her she didn't want to hear anymore and told her congrats on her upcoming wedding and she had to leave because her lunch break was almost over. She called me as soon as she left. She said can you believe it! As much as they were against me at least I graduated from college and have a thriving career and ministry. She said she couldn't help but to wonder if she would have married him if they would have been happy. She said she really loved him, but she had found out other girls had gotten abortions by him, and his parents gave him the money for it. She didn't know if they knew what he would be using the money for. And she said it made her think if his parents paid for hers? She said she really hadn't talked to her mom that much since she found out her cousin was really her older sister. But they may need to meet so she could get some clarification. I remember the scripture Darius said Malik's dad had given him about forgetting about the past and to press towards the mark for the prize of your high calling! I told her to remember what state of mind she was in when her parents dropped her off at school. How she end up telling me she thought about killing herself. I told her to do what this scripture says and don't go back to that place of betrayal, hurt and hate. To stay on track with the ministry God had given her. I told her, just think you already have a jump start on a thriving ministry you have already been on a local Christian radio station, the local news and have joined forces with a recovery center to get special funding for people that are being referred to PKID. She said you're right! And said that's why she is so thankful God had ordered our footsteps to be friends and work together in ministry. She said I was there for her when no one else was. I said you mean Jesus and me, we both just laughed. She said she hoped her old boyfriend would make it since his parents were so set on him being successful as a Pastor. I asked her if he ever told her that's what he wanted to be. She said he told her since he could remember that's all his parents ever talked about. His dad was a successful business man and back when his parents were coming up he told her churches felt like you had to give up everything to serve God, including your money. They had kids and his mom didn't work at first and they needed his dad's salary. I asked why him? He has brothers and sisters. One of his sisters is a great speaker, but they don't believe in female pastors. She was a great speaker at school people started to ask her to speak for different occasions. Lillian said he told her at first she wasn't going to preach at church because of her parents. But recently she has been accepting speaking engagements and she is on fire for God! She's been asked to speak at youth services and women's conferences. His sister said she kept feeling a nudging by God to go for it and she did! His parents had never even been to hear her speak. They put everything into her old boyfriend because he has the look, the voice and they believe he is the charismatic one out of the bunch. I said but what did God say? Did God even call or choose him for what they are directing him to do? She said she didn't know he just wanted to please his parents. I said but what about God?

Chapter 4

What About God?

It seems funny how some people just copy and plagiarize what other people are doing. Should we just do something because someone else or another ministry has done it?

One thing I have always noticed is how some parents are so manipulative when it comes to their children. I can't count the amount of kids I went to school with that were pursuing careers just because their parents said that's what they should do. I always asked is this what you want to do with the rest of your life. They said they were going to school for it because their parents were paying or helping them out. But will you be stuck with that type of job I always asked, no one had even thought what would happen once they got their degree. They were just happy to get away from home and attend college. But would they be happy when they started working in a field they had no desire to be in? I remember when I was younger every year my parents would have us do a vision board in January. I use to look back on some of them to see if I stuck with what I was saying. My parents gave me direction but I made my own choices and once I start going to church I always tried to find out what the will of God was for my life. And to work with Him not against Him!

This made me think of the amount of people I have known for years, even from the don't churches that don't even pray and read their bibles every day. It's amazing! They are so into the church service and looking the part but in 1st Samuel 16:7 it says man dwells on the outward appearance but God looks at your heart. What about God knowing you just look the part but may be living a loose life and doing the same thing you are judging sinners for doing. What about God in all these situations? I can't worry about everybody else, I have to work out my own salvation with fear and trembling and go on with my life. I pray that everyone makes it, but I'm in a race myself to finish until the end with God. Because

I'm aware the race is not given to the swift, nor battle to the strong, neither yet bread to the wise, nor yet riches to men of understanding, nor yet favor to men of skill; but time and chance happens to them all! I know I have my perfect time with God to be successful! Time and chance happens to us all! I have to seize the moment when it's my time and chance because no one lacks opportunity. I heard someone say everyone is given 24 hours in a day. It just depends on what you do with your 24 hours. I want to follow the plan of God for my life and not get off track. I thought as born again believers are we really concerned about the will of God, or is it more important to have a large membership. Is it more important to try to keep up with other people or find out if whatever it is, is it the will of God for you or your ministry. What about God? What about all the spiritual leaders in scandals? Yes we should forgive them, but what kind of example are they to younger people? I wonder why they are so hard on us when they are doing the same thing or worst. I guess they still old school it and say do what I say, not what I do, but they are suppose to be teaching younger people the right way to go according to the bible. I'm just trying to live each day thinking what about God! This has helped me so far in my spiritual walk because my parents didn't start going to church until I did. I'm not like some of my friends who went to church as baby's and getting dedicated. But I guess when I start going I was serious and always had that question on the inside of me. It seems like it has helped me make the right choices. I always think, What About God before committing to anything!

Chapter 5

Out There!

Darius and his team just went out on their first Saturday witnessing. Raquel wanted to give out food so they incorporated food with the help of Matt's parents. They had told Darius they would help him anyway they could so he called them on it. Raquel also wanted to bring one of her younger cousins that attended school here. She said it would help while witnessing to families that had kids when they saw other children. Luke had already ordered tracts in Spanish. Raquel got some Spanish bibles from her family to give to those that didn't have one in their home. Brittney did great witnessing to the kids with the help of Raquel and her cousin and before they would leave a home they gave the children candy. Brittney also told the adults she could help with papers if they needed any assistance, it seemed like they felt more at ease with Raquel being with us since she was Spanish. We couldn't believe how great everything turned out. But Darius did! He always had people coming to church every month from him witnessing and praying for people. Darius had told all of us the night we were at the shut in we would be using key scriptures. Some of us had to learn one on healing, some on salvation, some on forgiveness and some for just help in desperate times. It was working great because some of us remembered scriptures we had to learn in school and we tagged teamed it like on debate teams! We were so thankful we had translators when we went to homes where no one spoke in English. We were out for about an hour and witness to over 100 people including the kids. We were curious to see how many people would show up that we had invited to church. Darius said if only one came that's was one more than before! Brittney and Luke did go to lunch afterwards as he had promised her.

Brittney told her parents how she was able to make some contacts for her portfolio. Her mom told her she would be coming to church Sunday. To our surprise a couple of families did come.

After church Luke wanted to speak with Maliks dad and he asked him if we could start incorporating music in Spanish during the service. He said someone could start learning some songs and if the church needed to we would be ready to sing. Malik asked his dad if it could start being a service in Spanish if we needed one. His dad said we could meet and talk about it. We all met before going out that next Saturday. The pastor said he didn't believe in having separate services, was heaven separated by nationalities? We should all be worshipping God together. We would just use translators and sing whatever songs in both languages. We would be able to use Raquel and Brittney as translators when needed. And off the SSW team went again. We would also be composing Praise and Worship teams that could sing in Spanish. I was so happy about how things were moving so fast. Or were they? We had been getting trained for this since we were in middle school, the timing was right. This was our season!

After we went out witnessing Lillian and I joined Luke and Brittney for lunch and who did we run into, Lillian's old boyfriend! He was there brainstorming with the team he would be touring with. The next day at church we had people that visited again! We were thankful to see the fruit of our labor already. Later that day Lillian told me her old boyfriend contacted her and said he was sorry for everything and it was good seeing her again. She said he wanted to meet with her, but she told him she had moved on with her life and wished him the best. I told her I couldn't believe he was calling her! She told me it was easy to turn him down because she had been going out with a guy she had met at college that was part of our prayer service on Saturdays. She said she was going to invite him home for the 4th of July to her grandparents and she wanted him to meet my family. She said she wasn't going to introduce him to her parents or visit her old church. I told her I wouldn't either, but to make sure she has forgiveness for her parents and the church member's, don't let them hold her mind, heart or future in a prison in the present or future in her life! She said she knew and counseling others had become therapeutic for her as well! Things were moving right along. And our appointments were booming at PKID we needed new office space!

Chapter 6

NEWBIES

We went out looking for a small office space, but Lillian's grandparents said we could use one of their rental properties. It was empty and we could use it if we wanted it. It was a nice home, but needed some repairs and to be updated. We jumped on it because it was rent free! We asked some of our friends if they could help paint and get the yard together. We heard there were some remarks. Some counseling companies thought "the millennials didn't know what they were doing, and we were too young and didn't have any experience". We didn't have to prove anything to them we were just being led by the Holy Spirit. I suggested we rent out some of the space to some of our friends that had thought about starting some type of business. We approached Brittney because we heard her telling people when we were out witnessing she could help with papers. She accepted and when she told Luke he wanted to rent a room to be available to have 24 hour prayer anytime someone wanted to come and pray or needed prayer. They could come anytime, on their way to work, on a lunch break after work, whenever! Before we knew it all the rooms were sold! Brittney would share half of the basement with us it had a separate entrance and was divided into two separate areas. Luke took a bedroom and converted it for a prayer room, Raquel rented a bedroom and turned it into office space to be used as a tutor room for Spanish children that were in school and any adults that wanted to speak in English. And to our surprise Santiago wanted a room! We had met him in Honduras he helped transporting us. He was here on a visa. He would be using a room for an office space to train people in the stock market. He had gone to some Penny Stock classes and had made a quite a bit of money on the OTC. We decided to let him have the family room and gave Luke his room as a bedroom. We needed someone to be there at all times since Luke wanted the home to be available 24 hours for prayer. He made sure he would have someone scheduled at all times to be on the property.

All those that would be using the property for business joined in to get it ready. We planted flowers, painted it inside and out. Got new fixtures and we told everyone they had to have 1 month's rent in advance. Lillian and I used it to furnish our office area. Everyone was responsible for getting their area furnished. Santiago helped out a lot since he had made some money. He had the carpet taken up and had the hardwood floors refurbished. The kitchen was up-dated with counters and stools, and the bathroom was updated with a new shower put in. Lillian's grandmother said if we needed her to she would come over and cook sometime, we prayed about it and asked her if she could cook on Sundays before or after church to feed the hungry in the community. She agreed and to Brittney's surprise her mom said she would cook too once she found out! Her parents were so proud of her already being so active helping people and finding a church that was actually making a difference! Her dad said he never saw or heard of local churches being a part of the community like this. And he felt like the tv preachers just wanted to hoard up money for themselves. She didn't know it but he told Luke he was thinking about coming to church. Luke told him he could come over anytime and he would be more than happy to pray with him and for him. He told Luke he didn't know how to pray, Luke told him we all have to learn and even the disciples ask Jesus to teach them how to pray.

I was the PR person out of the group and I had contacted a local station telling them what we were teaming up doing and Lillian was the founder of PKID. I told them how she was on their station before when she had started her ministry and this was sort of Phase 2 to her vision. They came over while we were getting everything together and when we were having our grand opening. We were thankful there were no zoning issues for what we wanted to do. And before we knew it we were up and running. Luke suggested to SSW team to come over every Saturday before we would go out witnessing and most people did. There were some that just met us where we would be witnessing. Our group size had doubled because there were more children that wanted to go out too! After Luke and Brittney would go to lunch on Saturday's when they came back she would reserve time to helped Spanish students filling out papers to go to college. It seems like we newbies were off to a good Godly start!

Chapter 7

Are You Kidding Me!

Before the end of summer Lillian told me her old boyfriend had called and wanted her to meet with him. I said you're not thinking about meeting him are you? She said she felt like she should. I said are you kidding me! You know some kind of way this is going to backfire on you! But she said she kept feeling like she should talk with him. I told her to have him come over to our new location, but he wanted to meet at another location. I told her if she really wanted to meet with him I would go to. She set up the meeting and I went along. He wanted to meet at a coffee shop, she said no, so they met at a deli. She told him I was there. I didn't sit with them, but could tell he didn't like it. He told her he couldn't believe she didn't trust him. She said why should she? He told her he was sorry for what he put her through and wished he had never listened to his parents. She told him that was in the past, but when was he going to start making his own decisions? He told her that he found out his oldest son wasn't even his baby! And how he wanted to get a divorce, but both their parents were so against it and her parents didn't want anyone else knowing the oldest baby wasn't his. He said since the next 2 were his he stayed in the marriage.

Lillian asked him if he was sure the other ones were his? He said yes and the way his life was in a mess he had thought about suicide. He said he didn't know how God could forgive him for all he had done? She told him he knew what it said in Micah 7:19, He will turn again; he will have compassion upon us; he will subdue our iniquities; and thou will cast all their sins into the depths of the sea. They held hands and he repented and rededicated his life to Christ. It's not God's will for any man to perish. While this was going on someone from their old church walked in and saw them holding hands and took a picture and put it on FB. They didn't know what was going on but just wanted to start some mess! After Lillian prayed for him she motioned for me to come over and we prayed for him again. When the person from their old church saw us praying and saw what was really going on it was too late, her friends were already sharing the photo. And of course it got back to his wife.

When we left we went back to the office, her old boyfriend went home and to his surprise had to get in an argument with his wife as soon as he walked in! He didn't know what she was going off about until she showed him the picture. He told her he had asked Lillian to meet with him because he wanted to apologize about how he had treated her and that I was there at another table. He told his wife how he had rededicated his life to Christ and how we had prayed with him. She said she thought he was trying to get back with his old girlfriend. He said no he wanted to make the best of their marriage. He told her he was going on the tour since it was the last minute, but he wanted to do motivational speaking when he came back, and not just limited to the church. She said our parents may not be supportive, he told her he was tired of not doing what he wanted to do and what he believed God had put inside of him to do just to please his parents. He told her anyway he was just barely holding on to their marriage since he found out their oldest son was not his and who was the father anyway? She was outraged he bought this up, she started screaming and hollering and said maybe she should have married the father, she would have been happier! They weren't even thinking the children could hear them. Their oldest son walked in the room and asked if he was his father? His wife just burst into tears. Lillian's old boyfriend just got his suitcase and walked out the house to let his wife deal with it. While he was touring he got a call saying his son had killed himself. He was only six! We couldn't believe it! How could a six year old kill himself. We found out he had got a gun that was kept in the house and later that night he shot himself. But why would a six year old even be thinking about suicide? His mom of course blamed her husband for initiating the conversation and said he always treated him differently. No one knew he wasn't his son and everyone knew that wasn't true, him and his parents treated the oldest boy just as well as the younger two children that were his.

There were a lot of people we went to school with that came to the funeral. Most said they were shocked. People came that did not know him or his family. They just could not believe someone so young would take their own life, and the media was there. Lillian offered to go and talk to the students at his school and offered free counseling for any children that thought about suicide or had question for the next 2 weeks. We couldn't believe there were people showing up with their children. Lillian's old boyfriend filed for divorce from his wife, she begged him to stay in the marriage and asked if they could try counseling. She told him you went to see Lillian and now look at what a mess it has made. He told her he wasn't happy, and he never wanted to marry her, his parents forced him and Lillian didn't have anything to do with their son's death! He told her he would be moving out, she could stay in the property since their parents were paying most of the bills anyway. He told her he would find some kind of job until he got up on his feet to help with the kids. She called his parents and they came over to no avail. He couldn't believe how they were still trying to "protect" his image. He told them to let it go! Too much had happened he had repented and was going on with his life.

He went to get some gas and Malik was there too. He asked him if he could pray for him and he accepted and said he needed all the prayer he can get! He shared with him how he had rededicated his life to God and was filing for divorce. He told him he just really wanted to be a motivational speaker and to have a webinar talk show he never wanted to be a pastor. Malik told him he would be praying for him, but to think about the divorce. He knew a lot had happened. He told him just look at what happened when his son found out he really wasn't his father. And the remaining children already have to deal with the death of their brother, the parents arguing and not getting along and how would the divorce affect them? Did he want some other man raising his children, or them having to live with the grandparents and them raising them? He said he would think and pray about it while he was touring.

While he was touring one of the elders from their old church had gone over his house. I guess no one thought anything of it, and just assumed he was going over to pray. Until it was found out the oldest boy was his! He started an affair with Lillian's old boyfriend's wife when she was 17! His kid's were grown and he had grandchildren older than the boy that died.

They were so hard on the members and would not allow them to do anything or go anywhere and they were in church 3 and 4 days a week every week. But something like this still happened! I know there are true believers that are living by the bible. But I can't help thinking about how they thought they were so strong spiritually because in their mind they looked the part with all their tradition and no one knew their secrets. They need to read Mark 7:13, Making the word of God of none effect through your tradition, which ye have delivered: and many such like things do ye! Some of us were continuing to grow spiritually but there were quite a few of us that went to school together before we graduated that have already falling short. Not just at the don't churches, but all of them. As a matter of fact it was more that were living any kind a way without church and Jesus. And then you had the ones that were living crazy and still going to church almost daring someone to "judge" them and call them out on their sin nature because they said God is love. That doesn't give people the right to live any kind of way. I know if people repent and go on living a sinful life they may not realize it, but they are playing with fire. They will get burned with the Holy Ghost Fire! And some know this but are willing to take their chances. I can't believe the amount of people that got saved that summer at camp because of the fire that had just quit going to church. They said they will just try to repent before they die. But will they have a chance. In the bible God say's He comes back in a twinkling of an eye! I looked this up before. A twinkling of an eye is eleven one-hundredths of a second! I don't think they will make it, but for some reason numerous people are taking this route has gone down the toilet? We started out strong and were on fire for God but now our harvest has diminished!

Chapter 8

Diminished Harvest

I believe there is hope! God can still work with the remnant that is left! He promised us in Isaiah 11:5, "The remnant shall return, even the remnant of Jacob, unto the mighty God!" I believe not only shall we get a new harvest from the seeds we are planting going out witnessing, but a resurrected remnant from the harvest that has diminished! I don't know how people think they can survive without God. He wakes us up in the morning, not an alarm or a phone call, but God. With just a few of us trying to be available for God's service we are getting somewhere! I cannot help but to think where we would be in the body of Christ if everyone will work out in their vocation instead of thinking it is somebody else job or wanting to do somebody else's job instead of their own. It is much easier just going to church, not being involved and throwing some type of offering in. Are people satisfied with this or is it that they don't want to make the sacrifice to get to the next level spiritually. I'm young but I know anything worth having you have to work for. I'm also interested in winning souls and having our church membership grow. I remember what it says in Acts 16:5, "And so were the churches established in the faith, and increased in number daily."

This may be part of the problem. Are people being established in faith because faith comes by hearing and hearing by the word of God? Are people hearing the word of God when they attend church or are they hearing something else? Because God says when we hear the word of God our faith is suppose to be increased. And without faith we can't please God anyway. I was feeling strong in this area and couldn't let it go. It turned into a burden sort of speak. I start praying then fasting about a remnant. I questioned God about what I should do? Was praying and fasting enough? I felt that I should approach parents and grandparents of people that have stopped serving God, but how? I met with my pastor to inform him what I had in my heart and asked how could I get in touch with people? I told him I had been praying Jeremiah 31:16-17 everyday! "Thus saith the Lord; Refrain thy voice from weeping, and thine eyes from tears: for thy work shall be rewarded, saith the Lord; and they shall come again from the land of the enemy. And there is hope in the end, saith the Lord, that thy children shall come again to their own border!" He said it could be in our church announcements, they were shown on the screens before and after services, and I could have time before the offering to talk about it. We would have time before services to intercede on behalf for the lost and backsliders. Not to just use all of this time to socialize before the services got started. I said God can do a lot with 12 minutes. Twelve represents faith, the church and divine rule and God's power. We need God's power on it because without it we would be meeting for nothing! I was surprised and thankful there were a few grandparents that said they would come early before Sunday services to intercede for their family and others. It just may be that something would be happening after all with this Diminished Harvest!

Other Books by Dr. Wanda

Evangelism in The 1900's

Don't Work For The Money Let The Money Work For You!

The Harvest Is Past, The Summer Is Ended, And we Are Not Saved!

Can Somebody Tell Me Where The Altar Is?

Harvest Of The Remnant

Learning Both languages At The Same Time

When Healing Doesn't Come

Not By Might, Nor By Power, But By The Spirit of God!

The Servant That Wants To Be Served

My Vision Board

The Coward Bully

Forgive Me For Not Being A Hoe!

Contact Dr. Wanda on Facebook

Or

Knowledge by Dr. Wanda

Also

https://wandatolbert.netlify.app//